The Eco-Diary

of

Kiran Singer

The Eco-Diary
of
Kiran Singer

By Sue Ann Alderson

Illustrated by
Millie Ballance

Vancouver London

Published in 2007 in Canada and Great Britain by
Tradewind Books · www.tradewindbooks.com

Distribution and representation in Canada by
Publishers Group Canada · www.pgcbooks.ca

Distribution and representation in the UK by
Turnaround · www.turnaround-uk.com

Distribution and representation in the US by
Orca Book Publishers · www.orcabook.com

Book design by Jacqueline Wang
Cover design by Elisa Gutiérrez

Colour separations by Disc, Vancouver, BC
Printed in China on 100% ancient forest friendly paper.

10 9 8 7 6 5 4 3 2 1

Cataloguing-in-Publication Data for this book is available from The British Library.

Library and Archives Canada Cataloguing in Publication

Alderson, Sue Ann, 1940-
    The eco diary of Kirin Singer / by Sue Ann Alderson ; illustrated by
Millie Ballance.

Poems.
ISBN 978-1-896580-47-0

    1. Camosun Bog (Vancouver, B.C.)--Juvenile poetry. 2. Ecology--Juvenile
poetry. 3. Nature--Juvenile poetry. 4. Children's poetry, Canadian (English).
I. Ballance, Millie II. Title.

PS8551.L44E36 2007   jC811'.54   C2007-901347-3

The publisher acknowledges the support of
the Canada Council for the Arts.

 Canada Council   Conseil des Arts
for the Arts   du Canada

The publisher also wishes to thank the Government of British Columbia
for the financial support it has extended through the book publishing tax
credit program and the British Columbia Arts Council.

 BRITISH COLUMBIA
ARTS COUNCIL
Supported by the Province of British Columbia

The publisher also acknowledges the financial support of the Government
of Canada through the Book Publishing Industry Development Program
(BPIDP) and the Association for the Export of Canadian Books (AECB)
for our publishing activities.

 Canadä

Dedications

For my wonderful grandchildren,
Dag, Desiree and Henry,
with love from Grandma Sue

and

for my daughter, Rebecca,
my original Kiran

and

to the memory of my friend
Seepeetza (Shirley Sterling),
author of *My Name is Seepeetza*,
whose spirit I felt was with me
as I worked on this book

—S.A.A.

To Dan

—M.B.

Introduction

I first saw Camosun Bog when I was on a walk taking photographs in the woods of Vancouver's Pacific Spirit Park. I walked down a hill and the trees gave way to a bright clearing with a small pond. In the middle was a golden pond lily bud ready to burst into bloom. It was beautiful and peaceful, and I knew I would return to this special, tranquil pocket of wilderness.

During the summer of 2005, I spent some time visiting and working on the restoration of Camosun Bog. This book is the result of my experience on the bog and with the boggers.

Camosun Bog is an unusually small bog in an unusual locale—at the edge of a public park in the middle of Vancouver, British Columbia. People live a couple of blocks away. Yet it is ancient, dating back to the ice age.

The bog has remained, despite frequent attempts to fill it in over the years. However, thanks to the efforts of a group of volunteers who call themselves the Crazy Boggers, the Camosun Bog is thriving. The Crazy Boggers, officially known as the Camosun Bog Restoration Group, was organized by Laurence Brown and Brian Woodcock. Vancouver's Mayor Larry Campbell awarded the boggers the Mayor's Environmental Achievement Award for 2005.

More information on Camosun Bog can be found at the following web site: www.naturalhistory.bc.ca

If you would like to be involved in a similar environmental project, your local Natural History Club or Audubon Club will have all the information you need.

Acknowledgements

I owe thanks to many people for their support and for allowing me to use their stories in my poems. Thanks especially to Denis Underhill and Adam Snow. Thanks also to Kathy Gibler, Pat Wilson, Sonia Huzyk, Sig Techy, Issaku Inami, Shuhua Xu, Yi Luo and Brian Woodcock for their support.

Thanks to Jill Deuling for all the time she spent walking me around the bog and giving me the ecological viewpoint, including many details I have used in my poetry.

And a special thank you to Laurence Brown for his careful reading of my manuscript through many revisions, his stories and his warm support.

Dear Grandma,

Tsunamis
Hurricanes
Earthquakes
Disappearing rainforests
Melting glaciers
Pollution
Oil-spills
Nuclear waste
Terrorists
Wars

I think we live on the side
of a volcano. No one is safe.
We have to do something.
Sometimes I'm scared.

But what can I do?
I'm just a kid.
What can a kid do?

Love,
    Kiran

Dear Kiran,

Come with me to my work party this weekend. There's a bit of the planet right here practically in our backyard that needs looking after—it's a little bog. I think you will like it. And happy 12th birthday! I hope you like the present I'm giving you!

Love,
 Grandma

Dear Grandma,

Thank you so much for the diary! I know the perfect place to write—our little bog. I'll keep it all in poems about the things I hear and see and want to think about, and your stories too.

I love you,
 Kiran

Table of Contents

Sunday Morning

No car sounds today, just bird songs:
Chicka-dee-dee-dee! Twitter, chirp,
to-whee, to-whee!
Chicka-dee-dee-dee!
Wheee! Wheee!

Far off the city hums.
Near me, a quiet grey-haired woman finds
her footing for a Tai
Chi dance. Her arms circle, silent.

Louder LOUDER, an airplane passes,

                                  softer,

                                            softer,

                                                  gone.

Sun's over my shoulder,
the air still cool, the shadowed ground patched
with weak light.

My pen makes a tiny tapping on the t's.
My thumb slides over the paper—
shh, shh, shh.
I too am part of the morning song.

The Enchanted Bog and the Crazy Boggers

Once this bog was under an evil spell. The city
grew up around it. The bog fell asleep,
trampled, covered by debris.

Then one day the spell was broken.
People cleared away the trash, weeded
the moss, seeded, built walkways around it.

They call themselves the Crazy Boggers.
My grandma is a bogger. She weeds the moss,
the sun warming her back.
She's careful to save the baby
sundews, the labrador teas.
Her talk with friends blends
into the woodsy harmony.

I'd like to be a Crazy Bogger too.

Moss and Mud

Older than grandma,
older than the city,
thousands of years old,
our bog cleans the air.

Sphagnum moss is its heart—light green, dark green, soft red—
holds water like a sponge. Moss makes peat,
peat makes coal.

Sedges and rushes grow
from the mud at the edge
of the pond, wave in a
whisper of wind.
Their roots fold and hold
the wet earth together.

Yellow Pond Lily

Leaves float
'round a golden bud. These hearts will be
the rest-stop for a frog, the shade for creatures underneath.

Days pass. One blossom unfolds.
In the middle of the pool in the middle
of the bog, the lovely pond lily
imitates the sun.

Bog Walking

Stay on the boardwalk or walk on the rim!
Don't ever step in the bog
or the moss and the mud and the peat will suck
schlupp! schlupp! on your shoe
and you will be stuck.
The more you try to move your foot
schlupp! schlupp! schlupp! schlupp!
the further in you'll sink until
maybe you'll lose your shoe! I did that once!
I went back with a board to fetch it.
Am I ever careful now where I step!

Monday Noon

I'm back in the bog. Grandma's with me.
I hear a fly. A bee.
Eagles circle over head.

A tiny black ant crosses the boardwalk—what a hike!
Another ant investigates my leg—I give him the brush-off.

Eight dragonflies fly over the moss.
Almost as big as hummingbirds, they dart and hover—

       zip   zip   zip

No rain for twenty-three days.
The rain-fed pond is mud in the midst of brush.

Most of the bog is bright with sun.
The damselflies zip-zag over the reeds and rushes.

Eagle and Crows

Highest bird in the sky,
an eagle circles and circles,
seeking a nest to plunder.
He sees one,
      d
      r
      o
      p
      s like a rock.

Out of the trees comes a crowding of crows,
screaming and beating their wings,
together defending the nest
        and yes!
        up flies the eagle chased away
by the cloud of crows.

The baby birds, safe, open
their beaks and stretch their necks.

Dragonflies

Dragons breathed fire, but not dragonflies.
Why call them that? I don't know why.

Flying fast or slow, they hover and dart
and stop short!

Forward and backward in mid-air,
they're the best hunters, fly any old where!

To avoid the sun, the dragonfly
wraps his wings in front and hides.

He turns around and around
until he's standing almost upside-down!

Grandma's Raccoon

"What's this?" asks Grandma. "A vandal's been at work.
Moss has been torn up and left in heaps to die.
Who did this? Who?

"Aha! There he is! Masked,
as you might expect! It's Mr. Raccoon,
out for a munch of insects
that live under the moss.

"Go away, Mr. Raccoon! You can't tear up a bog
that way! Take off! Find something else to nibble on!"

But Mr. Raccoon doesn't run away.
He's not afraid of people, and **he does love bugs**!

"Don't worry, honey," says Grandma. "When the rains come
Mr. Raccoon will stop hunting in the bog.
Perhaps he'll find an umbrella somewhere
to hunt beneath. Or he'll be fond of
apples in someone's backyard."

Then we'll all say:
"Good luck to you, Mr. Raccoon! Good riddance!"

Grandma Sees a Douglas Squirrel

"Listen, honey," she says to me.
"Quick to the scamper,
quick to the warning *chirr*.
This little handful of fur
picks mushrooms in the fall,
dries them on the tree shelf
where the branch meets the trunk.
Then he hides them,
for the months of cold, the months when fresh food
is hard to find.

"This little handful of fur
is not like his cousin who nests in attics.
This one prefers the trees of the forest, the woodpecker holes,
the breeze and the sun when it comes.
This one knows about the wild mushrooms that grow
a rich harvest in the fall on the spongy moss."

Tuesday Early Afternoon

Diarytime.
The sun is hot and bright on the clearing.

Puta-puta-puta-put-put-put YEOWWWW!
Men with saws are cutting up stumps
to clear the ground for planting.
Puta-puta-puta-put-put-put YEOWWW!

When they're done,
we watch for smoke, Grandma and I.
We watch for fire. A fire in a bog
can burn underground for years.
A spark from the saw could start it—
it's been so hot and dry
the danger of fire is high.
We watch and wait.

Is that a crackle of flame in the bush?
No, it's only a bird.
Is that the swish of flame in the grass?
No, it's a passing snake.

The bog's safe today. No fire here.
They'll clear the cut up wood
in rumbling wheelbarrows.
They'll cart it away, return the bog
to insect hum and bird song.

Anna's Hummingbird

Tiny wings a blur,
the hummingbird sips sap
from a woodpecker's hole,
steals bugs from the webs of spiders,
builds her nest of spider webs and plant down.
She uses lichen to hide it, clever bird.
Beautiful, iridescent green,
hers is the sun-sparkle and the sun's sheen!

The Woods Around

The woods around the clearing
grow on old bog,
roots deep in the peat.
The earth is soft, springy as a mattress.
If you drop a heavy log,
it bounces.
Feel the earth shake?

Grandma Tells Me About Bog Laurel

The bog laurel can draw back
its stamen, taut like a bow.
Waiting for a bee to land exactly right,
its stamen lets go a load of pollen
for the bee to spread.
New seeds, new life.

Sundew

The tiny sparkling sundew plant
is an insect trap. Sticky beads
on tentacles on the leaves
glue the passing fly.
A leaf bends around it,
surrounds it,
digests it,
forgets it.

Wednesday, On the Way to the Bog

The sun lurks behind a cloud.
I pass a man hammering: bang! bang! bang!
He pulls moss from his grass.
In the bog, we pull grass from the moss.

Weeders, we people are.
Some are hammerers, or choppers or diggers.
Sometimes we're planters, we're keepers.
What else are we?

We may be sleepers, or weepers,
zeroes or heroes, yelpers and helpers,
menders and tenders,
and sometimes we're friends.

I'm at the bog.
Finally, the sun comes out from behind the cloud.

Tree Frogs

The bog used to be home to tree frogs,
green and small. But then an ogre
bull frog arrived and ate them all.

One day, when the pond dried to mud
and the tree frogs were gone,
the ogre disappeared.

Our class raised baby tree frogs in a pool
behind the school and brought them
to the bog. Gently we put each on a leaf.
This was a happy spell,
bringing back tree frogs to the bog.

Vole

A Cooper's hawk flies
over the clearing.
Danger!
Vole dives into her burrow.
She has runways, a room to store bulbs to eat in winter,
a nest for babies lined with grass and a back door
just in case. She waits a while. At last
she ventures out, has a chew of grass,
keeps one eye on the sky.

Grandma Talks of Slime Mold

In the fall you'll see
a gold or orange patch
come overnight and disappear the next:
a million cells together in a swarm—
no one knows why. It does no harm,
this bright splash of color coming and going
to its own rhythms, its own song.

Grandma Points Out a Dusky Shrew

"This tiny shrew can barely see.
He lives to eat. Hidden in the underbrush he sleeps
at most an hour at a time.
Then, by sunlight or starshine,
he sniffs out bugs
or earthworms or slugs.
This is how he spends his time
on earth."

"When he's asleep," I ask,
"does he dream of meals that are
plentiful and easy to find? Does he dream
of the beautiful fragrance?"

Thursday Late Afternoon

Half the bog's in shadow;
still, insects hum and birds call.

Two dogs pant as they pass:
hah, hah, hah!
Toenails tap-dance on the boardwalk—
Otis and Oscar rush for a sniff.

Frog calls—is the bullfrog back?
Just for a visit? Or passing through?

A shaggy little white dog pulls a girl
along the walk. This must be the hour
for dogs through the bog.

Two bikers chat as they go by.

Dogs and bikers
and trikers and wheelchairs too,
talkers and walkers and runners,
skip-to-my-lou prancers and dancers,

        hip-hoppers, flip-floppers

                and any old dance you

                      want to do!

Grandma Tells a Story about a Barred Owl

High in a tree, a young owl
swivelled his neck, hoping for
a glimpse of mice. He flexed
his wings, preened,
shrugged, then saw
something moving, bouncing, hippity-hop-hopping along,
so he swooped down,

> down,

> > down to grab hold—

of a young girl's ponytail!
Blech! Blech!

Silly young owl, back
on his branch
with a beak full of hair,
swiveled his head, still
in hope, still
in hope of mice.

Woodpecker

Tap-tap-tapping from
tall trees at the rim of the bog,
sharp beak strikes, drills holes in the bark,
feet holding tight, head forth and back,
hardly a breath between the stutter
of rap-rap-rapping.

Now a woodpecker plays the metal plate
at the top of a power-pole—
what a drumming is here!
He's saying to other woodpeckers, "Stay back! Stay away!
This is *my* bog today!"

Grandma's Story about Adam and the Velvet Leaf Blueberry

Velvet blueberry is an old timer.
Folks thought it died out,
disappeared like the dinosaurs.
But Adam was walking the edge of the bog one day
and found a single plant of velvet leaf blueberry.
Just one by itself.

He took cuttings and nursed them,
watched them and watered them,
gave them good bog soil.
One by one they grew roots and leaves
to thrive in the sun.

Grandma's Story about Denis and the Camosun Blueberry

Denis found a berry unlike any other—
dark red and sweet. He marked eleven plants,
studied them, took their measure.
To his pleasure, he discovered he had found
a brand new plant no one had seen before.
It's called the Camosun Blueberry,
named after the bog where it was found.

Friday Night, with Grandma in the Bog

No song-birds now.
The evening's dark and almost cold.

Small brown bats skim the clearing.

A Barred Owl calls:
"Who cooks for you-oo? Who cooks for you-oo?"

Coyotes yodel.

The full moon hangs low in the eastern sky,
white with a light halo,
masked by the branches of trees.
I see the man-in-the-moon's face:
eyes, nose and smile.

Small creatures go underground, deep.
Safe in their cozy burrows, they breathe in
the scent of warm honey earth
and sleep.

Grandma's Story about the Little Brown Bat

When mother bats are broody,
they band together in a cave or hollow tree,
make a nursery, fly with their pups holding on for a week or two,
then say, "Hey, little one! You're too big to carry now!"

They hang the pups up, upside-down and whisper,
"Hang around here while we go out for dinner, have six
hundred mosquitoes
or so. We'll be back." And back they come,
find their upside-down pups, by scent and sound.

In another week, the little ones are ready to fly,
soaring and gliding and dipping,
with a zig and a zag and a zig-zag-zag.
The baby bat is free and on the wing.

With a voice so high she can't be heard by human ears,
she sings.

Flying Squirrel

The flying squirrel doesn't fly.
She glides from branch to branch,
sleeps all day, feeds and plays at night.
She nests in hollows and woodpecker holes,
moves from nest to nest, sharing them as she goes.

She's a high-diving, sky-gliding, dare-devil—
that's the flying squirrel!

Coyote

At the edge of the bog
the silent coyote
a statue
does not move
does not flick an ear.
Suddenly
he's off
gracefully skims the surface of the wet moss
between berry bushes
behind a pine tree
disappears.

Saturday Morning

Lots of talk this bright day—sounds like a party!

Here are Grandma's friends, Sig and Denis, clearing leaves.
Laurence and Adam tote stumps.
Pat is shearing grass.
My friends dig.

Grandma and I are weeding.
If tiny curls of moss come up with the roots,
we carefully press them
into the wet earth.

When we're hot and tired out,
we have a tea break.
Yi tells me a Chinese story. I read some poems aloud,
Issaku likes them.
Kathy passes 'round cold chai,
tastes like cinnamon and nutmeg.

Laurence gives out badges
to the new boggers—including me!
The badge is a slice of pine that says,
"I'm a crazy bogger!"
And I am!

This is a good party, growing the bog.

Grandma Remembers Seepeetza's Teaching: First Nations People and the Bog

My friend Seepeetza taught me about her people.

First Peoples stopping
in this clearing in the woods
stepped softly on the bog,
gathered berries and Labrador Tea,
used the moss for diapers and bandages.
They took the tasty Yellow Pond Lily seeds
for popping.

First Peoples used the bog wisely and well.
They let it be.

Grandma Tells Denis's Story about the Hockey Puck

Many years ago, the bog and pond were huge.
In summer, Denis tried to pole a raft.
Guess what!
He couldn't touch the bottom.
Maybe the pond went straight through the world to the other side?

In winter, Denis and his friends skated on the pond,
played hockey.
Guess what!
One day they lost the puck.
Looked and looked and couldn't find it.
Did folks on the other side of the world play hockey too?

Last year, Denis was weeding the cloudberries. His fingers
came upon
something hard and round.
Guess what!
Carefully he separated
the sedges, the branches, the twigs, the leaves.
Denis found his old hockey puck just waiting for a game!

Bushtits

A flock of foraging bushtits
move quickly and chatter as they go.

They help each other build
their long, hanging nests in the bog:
grass and leaves and twigs are tied
with the silken threads of
spider webs, and lined
with flowers, feathers, hair.
Some say the nest looks like an old sock hanging there!

Bushtits sit on each other's eggs
and feed their young together.
In winter they crowd in a huddle to keep warm.
In the morning sun, they share their song.

Like a Poem

Our bog needs loving,
our bog needs care.
We crazy boggers
all share the work
like bushtits
building a nest.
We weave the bog together
like a poem
to keep it here
for everyone
forever.

One Plus One

One plus one plus one and so on
all working together.
That's how we can save something,
heal something, change something—
one plus one plus one, and so on.

One bit of the earth plus another bit of the earth plus another.
Together we'll figure out how.
There is no rule book.
If something doesn't work, we'll try
something else, until
we get it right.

Everyone can be part of the song, part of the poem:
this I know.

Sue Ann Alderson

Sue Ann Alderson was born in New York in 1940 and moved to Vancouver, BC in 1967, where she has lived happily ever after. She was a professor in the University of British Columbia's Creative Writing Program and has had 17 books published for children. She also writes poetry for adults which has been published in journals in Canada, Ireland and the United States.

Millie Ballance

Millie is originally from England. She studied at Heatherlys School of Art and Camberwell School of Art in London. She now lives and paints in Vancouver.

7/22/09